For Ella, in memory of May,
her grandmother — C. A. D.
For Lorna — Rob Ryan

Barefoot Books
2067 Massachusetts Ave
Cambridge, MA 02140

First published in the United States of America in 2010 by
Barefoot Books Inc

This book has been printed and bound in China
by Hung Hing Off-Set Printing Ltd
on 100% acid-free paper

Reproduction by B & P International, Hong Kong

This book was typeset in Twilight and Nordik
The illustrations were handcut from single sheets of paper,
individually colored by spray paint and photographed

ISBN 978-1-84686-355-4

Library of Congress Cataloging-in-Publication Data
is available under LCCN 2008051069

1 3 5 7 9 8 6 4 2

THE GIFT

CAROL ANN DUFFY
AND
ROB RYAN

Barefoot Books
Celebrating Art and Story

A LONG TIME AGO,

when the world and everything
in it was younger, there lived
a beautiful girl.

The girl lived in a small town with her mother and father. It was a quiet town, of a sort not found nowadays, and its sounds were church bells, children, cattle passing at the crossroads, boots on cobblestones, an accordion or a fiddle through the open window of an inn, the wordless voices of dogs, cats and, at nighttime, owls.

Before she went to sleep, she would look out across the moon-oiled rooftops of the small town toward the dark woods at its edge, listening to the gentle query of an owl and wondering what her life would bring.

One day, in early summer, the girl
and her mother and father were
picnicking in the woods. The girl had started
to make a necklace of buttercups and daisies.
She wandered between the trees collecting her small
flowers. She reached a little clearing, where buttercups
sparkled in the sunlight.

The girl knelt to continue her chain of flowers. She
could hear the murmur of her parents' voices nearby
as she pierced neat slits with her thumb and fingernail
into the soft green stems of the buttercups.

Bees prayed for honey at a wild rose bush. A thought suddenly came to the girl — as urgent and vivid as

a butterfly opening its orange wings — that she wanted
to be buried in this plot of land when she died.

No sooner had she had this strange, intense thought than there
was a rustle from the bushes and an old woman stood before her.
The woman, though lined with age and silver-haired, had a
strong and lovely face and her bright, watery eyes were kind. She
was barefooted and dressed in a long white robe.

"Give me your flower necklace," she said to the girl, "and you
shall have your wish."
The girl was alarmed at this and got to her feet.
"What wish?" she said.
"The wish to be buried in this plot of land when you die."
The girl stared as the old woman slowly sat down on the grass,
gazed up at her, and said again:
"Give me the necklace and you shall have your wish."

The girl looked at the
chain of flowers in her hands.
Quickly, she made a final piercing and
joined the two ends of the necklace together.

Then she took three swift steps toward the old
woman and looped the necklace around her neck.
As she did this, the girl heard her mother's voice calling
her name and looked behind her — and when she
looked back again, the old woman was gone. The
girl turned and ran through the trees.

By the time the picnic was over, the girl had
started and finished another flower chain
and she said nothing to her parents
about the old woman.

Time passed slowly and the girl was often in the woods with her family or with her friends. Whenever she was there, she would wander off on her own and spend a few minutes in the little clearing. If she had found a special stone, she would bring it to the clearing and place it there.

Once, she came with a pocketful of bulbs from home to plant — and they would be snowdrops. Another time, she came with a twist of paper with some seeds inside and planted them. They would grow into forget-me-nots.

And as the girl grew into a young woman, the plot of land began to fill with the loveliest flowers, the most fragrant herbs, and the most perfect stones.

The young woman had art in her hands and she became a painter.
She had her own small house in the town now and worked there in
a room generous with light. In the evenings, she walked through
the town to her parents' house or to her friends' houses. She had
love in her heart and fell for a friend of a friend of a friend.

Soon enough she moved to a bigger house in the town with him.
She had a child in her belly, and by the year's end, she was a mother,
painting her pictures as her child slept in a crib next to the easel.
Time passed slowly and brought many people who wanted to buy a
painting. Another child was born.

The woman visited the woods many times with her children. She still went to the clearing and tended the plot of land as her children played hide-and-seek among the trees.

Sometimes she brought her paints and canvas and painted there and these paintings were amazing in their intense use of color.

Time passed, and one winter, the woman's mother died and then her father. This was a season of real darkness for the woman. She painted nothing and kept her family close, as snow whirled and shredded itself around the house. But when spring came, she went again to the plot of land in the clearing in the woods, with a trowel and a packet of seeds.

The woman's life brought happiness in love and art, and her children grew and flourished. In time, they moved to their own houses in the town and, before she knew it, the older woman was a grandmother.

She took her grandchildren for walks in the woods and when they gave her a special stone or a pebble, she made sure to take it to the clearing and place it there.

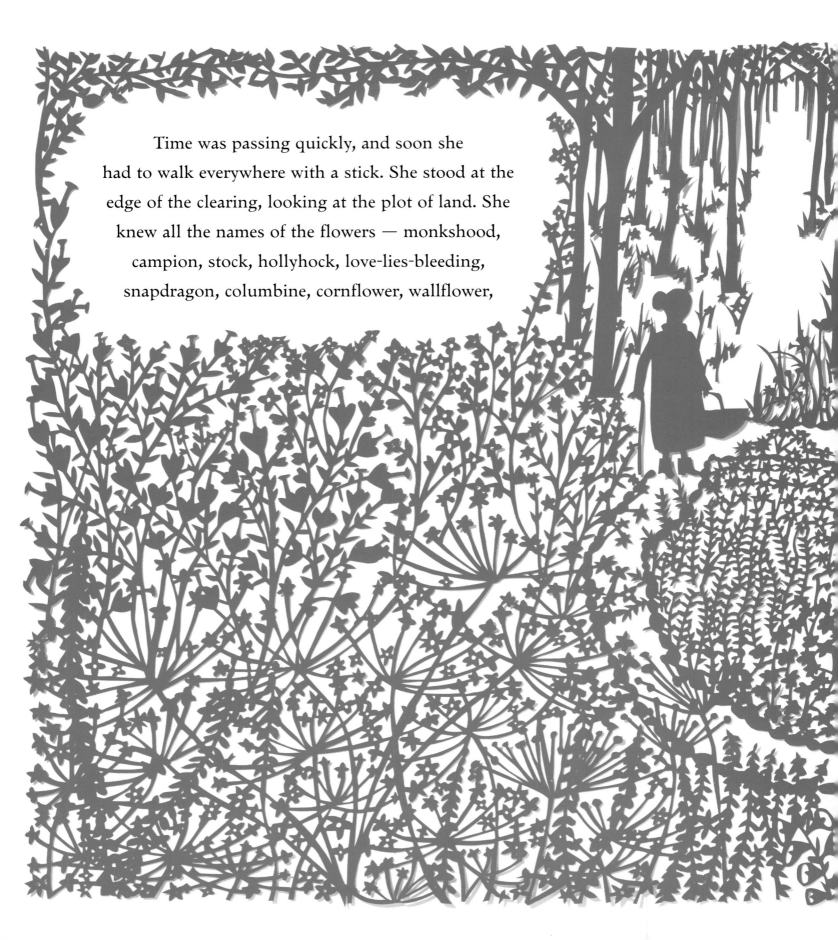

Time was passing quickly, and soon she
had to walk everywhere with a stick. She stood at the
edge of the clearing, looking at the plot of land. She
knew all the names of the flowers — monkshood,
campion, stock, hollyhock, love-lies-bleeding,
snapdragon, columbine, cornflower, wallflower,

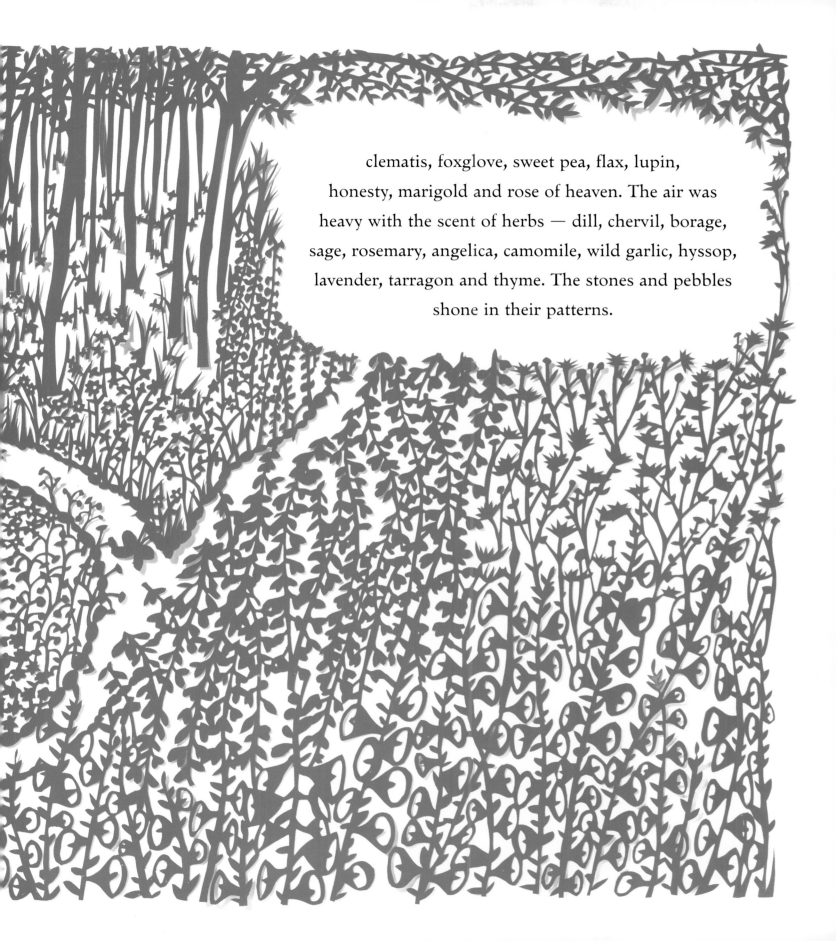

clematis, foxglove, sweet pea, flax, lupin,
honesty, marigold and rose of heaven. The air was
heavy with the scent of herbs — dill, chervil, borage,
sage, rosemary, angelica, camomile, wild garlic, hyssop,
lavender, tarragon and thyme. The stones and pebbles
shone in their patterns.

One day, even the stick could
not help the old woman to
walk, and her new painting
lay unfinished on the easel.

She grew weak and her family
gathered around, talking quietly,
and her grandchildren drew pictures
to pin on the wall by her bedside.

The old woman felt no fear and told her family that if anything happened, she wished to be buried in the plot of land in the clearing in the woods. She drifted into sleep and dreamed that she stood in the clearing again in her nightdress.

A young girl knelt there, making a chain of small flowers. She sat on the cool grass and the child stood up and stepped toward the old woman to place the flower necklace around her neck.

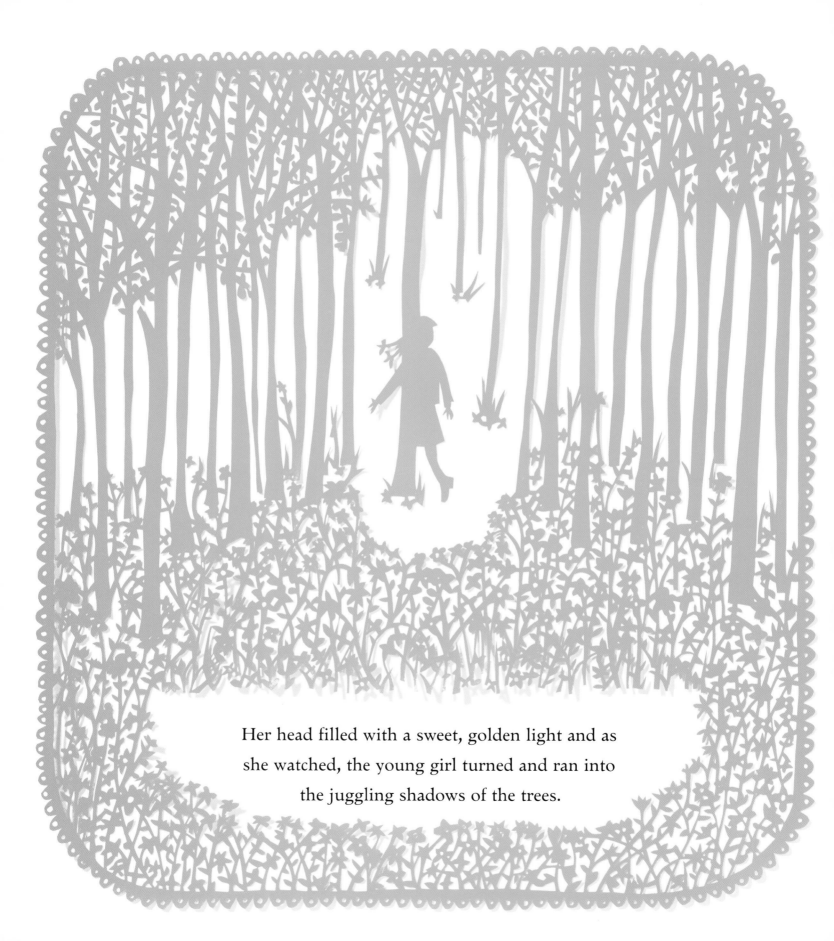

Her head filled with a sweet, golden light and as
she watched, the young girl turned and ran into
the juggling shadows of the trees.

Barefoot Books
Celebrating Art and Story

At Barefoot Books, we celebrate art and story that opens
the hearts and minds of children from all walks of life, inspiring
them to read deeper, search further, and explore their own creative gifts.
Taking our inspiration from many different cultures, we focus on themes that
encourage independence of spirit, enthusiasm for learning, and sharing of
the world's diversity. Interactive, playful and beautiful, our products
combine the best of the present with the best of the past to
educate our children as the caretakers of tomorrow.

Live Barefoot!
Join us at **www.barefootbooks.com**